BUILDERS & BREAKERS

First published in Great Britain 2019 by Walker Books Ltd, 87 Vauxhall Walk, London SE11 5HJ • © 2018 Steve Light • The right of Steve Light to be identified as author and illustrator of this work has been asserted by him in accordance with the Copyright, Designs and Patents Act 1988 • This book has been typeset in Egyptienne • Printed in China • • British Library Cataloguing in Publication Data: a catalogue record for this book is available from the British Library • ISBN 978-1-4063-8496-3 • www.walker.co.uk • 10 9 8 7 6 5 4 3 2 1

To Richard Binder, the best engineer I know.
May you always break the rules and build wonders.

BUILDERS & BREAKERS

STEVE LIGHT

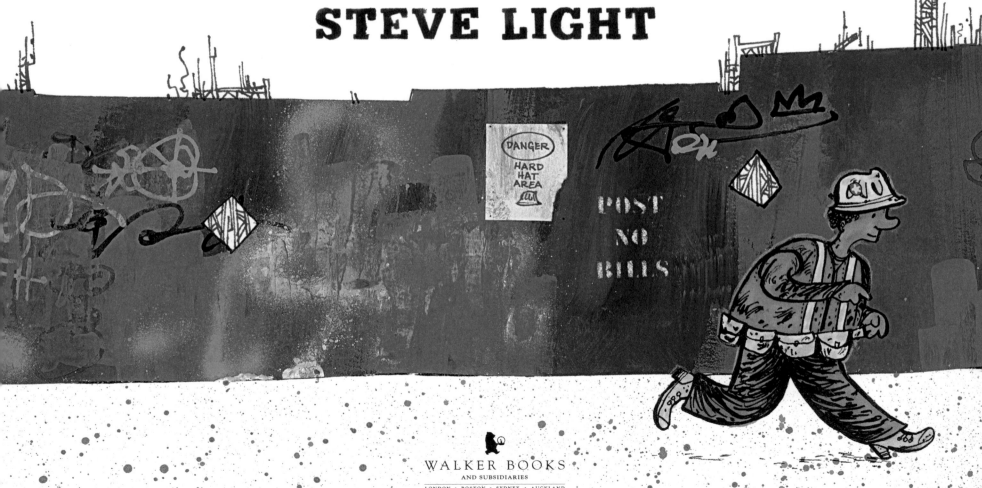

WALKER BOOKS
AND SUBSIDIARIES
LONDON · BOSTON · SYDNEY · AUCKLAND

Builders build

Breakers break

Build

Builder

Building

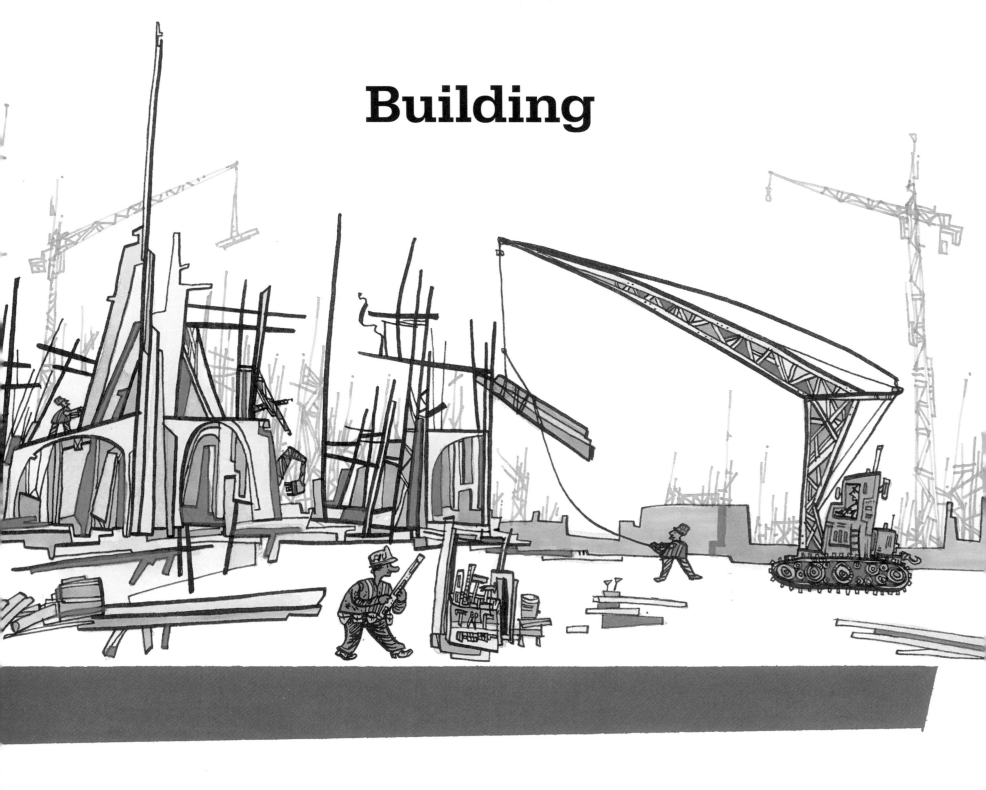

Break

Breaker

Breakthrough

Builders hammer

bang bang bang

Breakers jackhammer

rat-a-tat-tat-tat

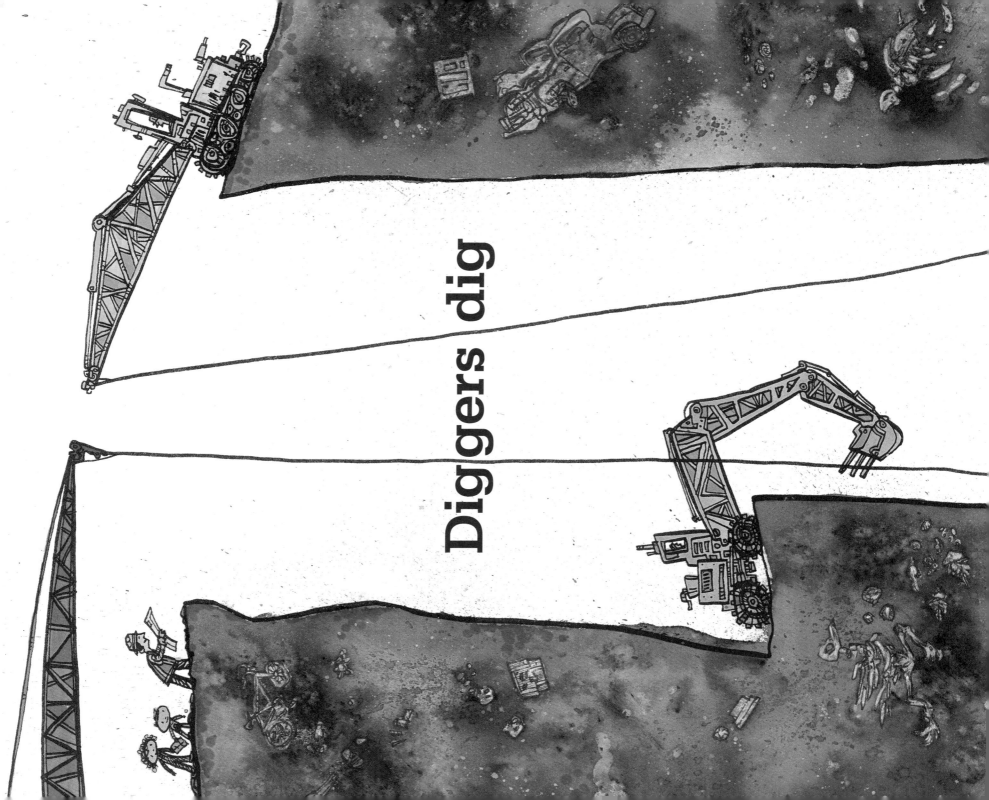

Diggers dig

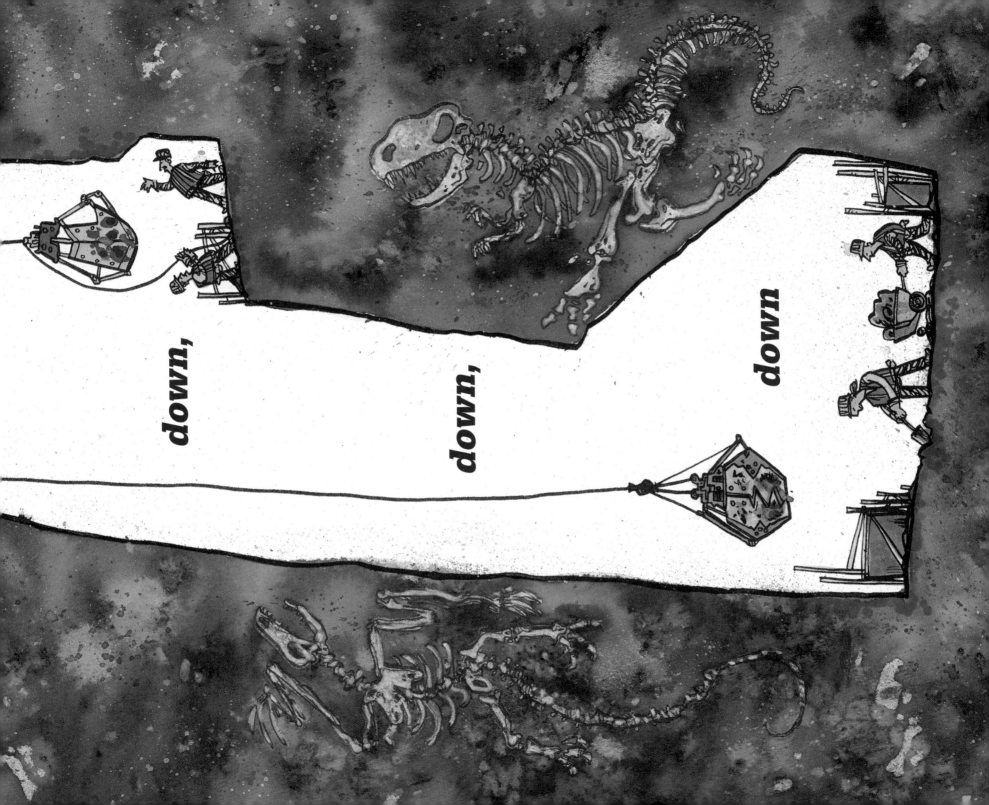

down,

down,

down

Welders weld

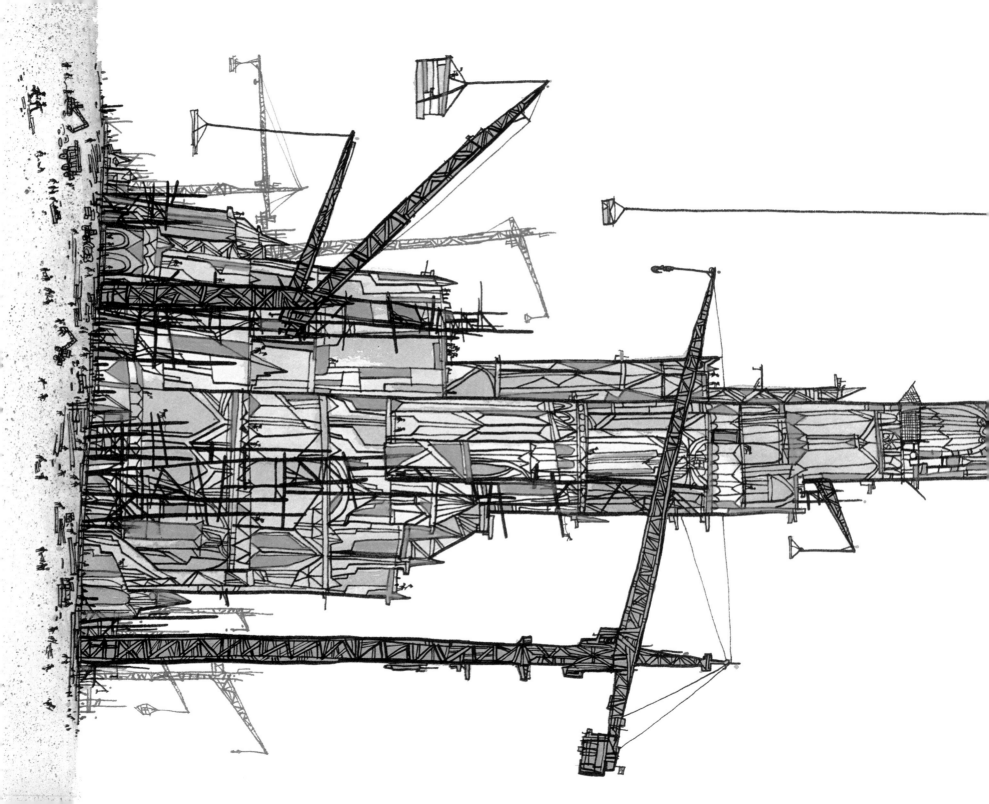

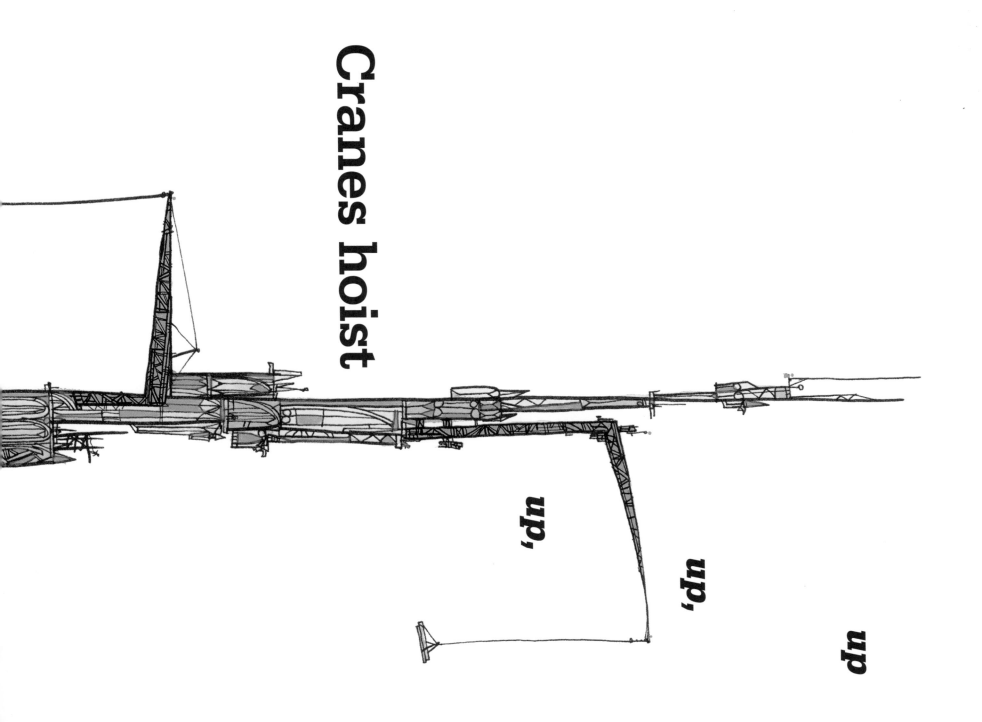

Cranes hoist

up, up, up up

Children search

look, look, look

Wheelbarrows carry

roll, roll, roll

After build time ...

comes break time.

AUTHOR'S NOTE

Builders could not build without breakers to clear the way. Breakers could not clear the way without the builders' plan. It is a relationship that lets buildings be created and cities grow.

All the architecture in this book is drawn from my imagination. The designs of these buildings are pure flights of fancy. I did, however, find inspiration in classical, Gothic and art deco architecture. I am fascinated

by the domes in classical architecture, the flying buttresses of the Gothic period, and the beautiful geometric designs from art deco. All of these combined in my imagination. The results are buildings that I dream about.

To build anything, something else must be broken, even if it's just ground. It is this balance – destroying in order to create – that, we hope, leaves us with something of beauty.

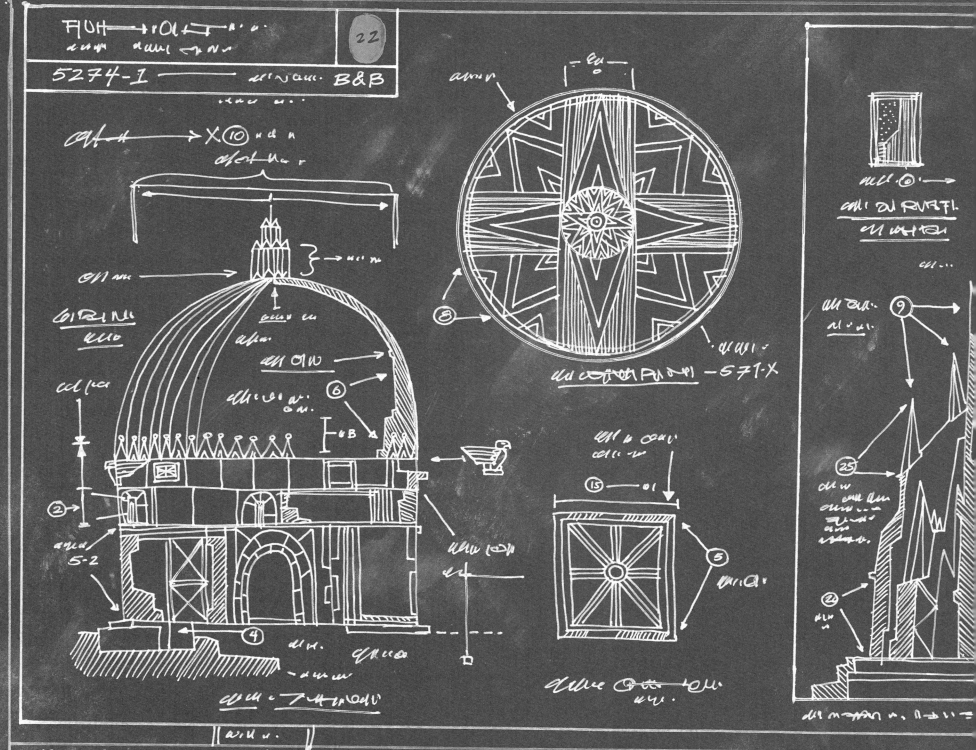